"Ahoy there, lads!" Mr. Krabs called out. "I have an idea about how we can get everyone to know about the Krusty Krab: by starting a Krusty Krab soccer team! And Squidward here is going to be the team's captain."

Squidward's mouth fell open. "Why me, Mr. Krabs?"

Mr. Krabs chuckled. "Because you have the most legs!"

At the soccer field Squidward waited for players to show up for the tryouts.

"Ah, soccer, the sport of people with real class," Squidward said to himself. He started to bounce the ball on his knees, but dropped it. Still Squidward was unfazed. "Yes, with twice as many feet as the other players, I'll be unstoppable! Now all I need are some teammates . . ."

Just then SpongeBob and Patrick ran onto the field. SpongeBob was calling, "I'm ready! I'm ready! I'm ready!" and Patrick was chanting, "Soccer! Soccer! Soccer!"

Squidward scowled. "What are you two barnacle brains doing here?"

"Trying out for your soccer team, captain!" SpongeBob replied, stopping in front of Squidward, who shook his head.

"Oh, lucky me," Squidward said.

Patrick looked around. "Hey, we're the only ones here! We're sure to get on the team!"

Squidward scowled. He did *not* want SpongeBob and Patrick on his team. "Do you two even know how to play the game?"

When SpongeBob and Patrick both shook their heads no, Squidward smiled. There's no way they'll pass this tryout, he thought.

"Great players have complete control when they kick the soccer ball," Squidward said. "You can bend it like David Barracuda or flick it like Mia Hammerhead, but the point is to put the ball into the goal. And it's not as easy as it—"

"Like this?" asked Patrick, kicking the ball all the way down the field and into the net.

Squidward's jaw dropped. "How did you do that? You haven't even learned how to dribble, or juggle the ball, or—"

"My turn!" SpongeBob yelled as he kicked the ball the length of the field into the other goal. "*Goooooaaaaaallllllll!*"

Squidward snatched up the ball. "Stop kicking goals! You're not ready for that! Look, it's easy to kick goals when no one's playing defense. But you've got to have a move that'll baffle the defenders."

SpongeBob was taking notes. "Baffle . . . defenders," he muttered to himself.

Squidward tossed the ball high in the air. "Watch my dazzling quadruple scissor kick. What do you think the other team will do when they see *this?*"

He flung his feet over his head, trying to kick the ball as it came down, but missed. His legs got tangled up, and he fell on the ground with a *thud!*

"Celebrate?" asked Patrick.

Squidward growled.

SpongeBob raised his hand. "Captain Squidward, don't we need more players for a soccer team?"

"Yes," admitted Squidward, "but I have no idea how to get them."

SpongeBob went to Goo Lagoon to see his friend Larry the Lobster. Larry was great at all kinds of sports like volleyball and weightlifting, so SpongeBob figured he would make a good soccer player.

"Hi, Larry," SpongeBob called. "Want to join a soccer team?"

"Soccer? How do you play it?" asked Larry, lifting a heavy barbell.

"Well," replied SpongeBob, "it's kind of like volleyball, only instead of using your hands, you use your feet. And instead of hitting the ball over the net, you kick it *into* the net."

"Hmm . . . sounds confusing," Larry said. "Count me in!"

SpongeBob got Pearl to be the team's goalie. She was very good at blocking kicks because she filled up most of the goal.

He also asked Sandy to join the team because she was terrific at every sport she ever tried.

"Yeehaw!" she yelled as she made a perfect bicycle kick. "I love this game, SpongeBob!"

Squidward watched SpongeBob practice with his friends. They're acting like SpongeBob is the captain of this team! he thought. I have to get back in charge—but how?

Then he had an idea. He would schedule the team's first game! Once everyone saw his spectacular moves, they would all look up to him!

By the day of the match Squidward had gathered enough players to make a full team.

"Where did you get the other players?" Patrick asked.

"Oh, they're good friends of mine who joined the team out of deep devotion and loyalty to me," Squidward answered.

Then one of the new players shouted, "Hey, what's-your-nose! Remember, you promised to clean our houses for a year!"

Plankton arrived with his Chum Bucket team. "We will destroy you!" he crowed. All of his players looked superfit, and they could do lots of tricks—bouncing the soccer balls off their feet, heads, knees, and backs.

"Gee," SpongeBob said nervously, "they look hard to beat."

But Sandy wasn't scared. "Look," she said, "we can win if we work together as a team! That's the secret to good sports play!"

"Team, team, team, team!" Patrick shouted, pumping a fist in the air.

Sandy was right. By playing as a team SpongeBob and his friends were able to keep up with their Chum Bucket opponents.

"I scored a goal!" SpongeBob shouted happily.

"And I got this neat yellow card!" said Patrick.

"Um, Patrick?" SpongeBob replied. "A yellow card isn't good. It's a warning—"

"No time for explanations!" Patrick said, running off. "Our team needs us!"

With only a few seconds left in the game, the score was tied. And the Chum Bucket team had control of the ball!

Suddenly Sandy was able to steal the ball and pass it through the other player's legs to SpongeBob! He ran down the field toward the goal as fast as he could, dribbling the ball with his feet.

"Shoot it, SpongeBob!" Larry yelled. "Shoot it!"

SpongeBob was about to take his shot. I'll win the game! he thought. I'll be the hero!

But then he spotted Squidward. "I'm open!" Squidward yelled, waving his hands frantically. SpongeBob hesitated. . . .

But then he remembered what Sandy had said about being a team player. Instead of kicking the ball toward the goal, he passed it to Squidward.

"*Nooooooo!*" screamed Patrick.

The ball was in the air. Squidward flipped himself upside-down and aimed all four of his feet at the ball. It was his special quadruple scissor kick, which he had never done right—not even once!

Squidward's upside-down spinning kick made the Chum Bucket goalie dizzy, and he lost track of the ball. The ball sped toward the goal, and—*Floomph!*—soared into the net!

"*Gooooooaaaaaalllllll!*" SpongeBob called. Squidward had won the game for his team!

SpongeBob watched the crowd carry Squidward off on their shoulders.

"That's funny," SpongeBob said as Larry walked up to him.

"What is?" Larry asked.

"I feel even better than if I had scored that goal myself!" SpongeBob said.

Larry shook his head. "I told you this game is confusing."